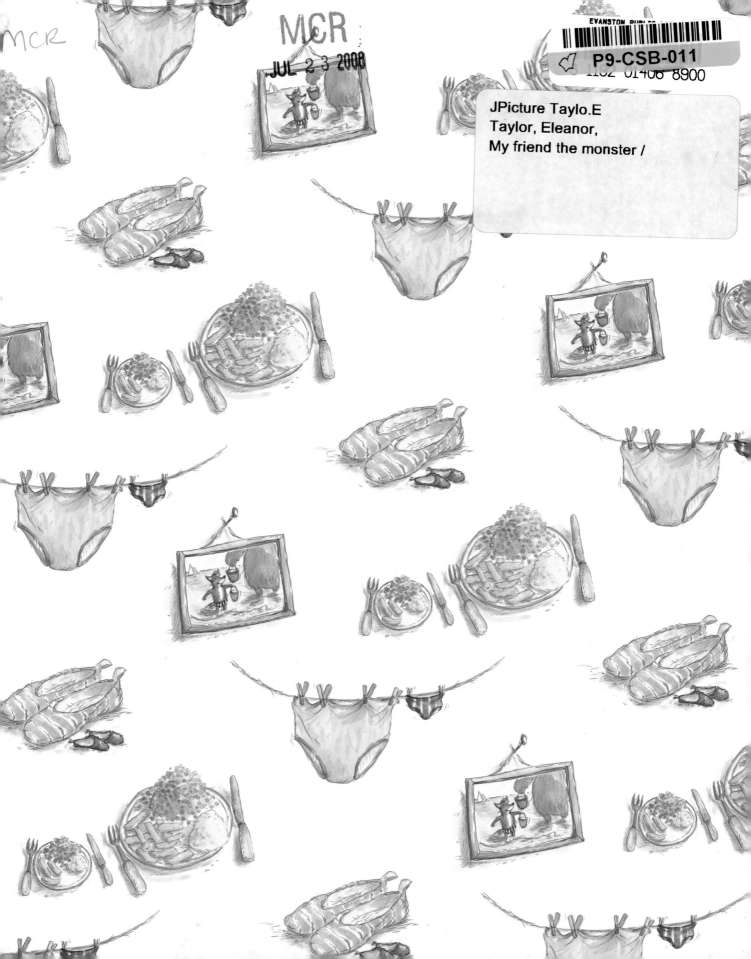

This book is dedicated to
Louis & Lola

Typeset in Whackadoo
Art created with watercolor

First published in Great Britain in 2008 by Bloomsbury Publishing Plc.
Published in the United States in 2008 by Bloomsbury U.S.A. Children's Books
175 Fifth Avenue, New York, NY 10010
Distributed to the trade by Macmillan

Library of Congress Cataloging-in-Publication Data
Taylor, Eleanor.
My friend the monster / Eleanor Taylor. — 1st U.S. ed.
p.   cm.
Summary: After his family moves into their new house, Louis the fox discovers a very
frightened monster living under his bed, and when he takes the monster to the park with
him, the monster helps him make new friends.
ISBN-13: 978-1-59990-232-6 · ISBN-10: 1-59990-232-X
[1. Foxes—Fiction. 2. Monsters—Fiction. 3. Moving, Household—Fiction.
4. Friendship—Fiction.] I. Title.
PZ7.T21258My 2008   [E]—dc22   2007044482

First U.S. Edition 2008
Printed in Malaysia
1 3 5 7 9 10 8 6 4 2

My Friend the Monster

Eleanor Taylor

BLOOMSBURY
CHILDREN'S
BOOKS

Louis and his family had moved to a new house. It was big and dusty and very quiet.

Louis ran from room to room shouting "boo!" into the empty closets. He listened to his echo in the attic and shouted "boo!" into the empty closet in his new bedroom.

That night Louis was awakened by a strange noise.
It was coming from under his bed.

"What are you, and why are you under my bed?" demanded Louis.

"W-w-well, I live here," blubbered the monster. "You woke me up with all that banging and shouting and drilling. Things have always been so quiet around here.

Now I'm cold and I'm scared, and I suppose that's why I'm under your bed."

Louis wasn't sure what to do. He had never had a monster under his bed before. "Please calm down," he said.

"But I'm scared," said the monster.

"Aren't you supposed to scare *me* if you're a real monster?" asked Louis in disbelief.

"Monster! Where? Oh, I'm terrified of monsters!" shrieked the monster.

"Please can I climb in with you? I've never really liked the dark," sobbed the blotchy-eyed creature.

"You won't wiggle or take all the blankets or snore?" asked Louis.

"Promise," snorted the monster.

"Thank you, Louis! Nobody has ever noticed me before," said the monster.

Then he yawned. "Wow, this is comfy, isn't it?" And with that he was fast asleep, wiggling, with all the blankets, and snoring like a train.

At breakfast, Louis tried to explain
to his family about the monster.

"I think he must have been left behind," said Louis.
"Nobody noticed me, is more like it," mumbled the monster.

Louis continued. "He probably shouldn't still be here, but he is. So now he will be my monster." Louis patted his monster's paw.

When Louis went to the playground for the first time, he decided to take his monster with him.

"Come on, my monster, we don't want to be late!" encouraged Louis.

On their way to the playground, Louis's mom wasn't sure which path to take.

So the monster put Louis on his shoulders.

From so high up, Louis could see the playground,

and he showed them which way to go.

At the playground, everyone stared at the monster.
He didn't know anyone's name and was afraid to ask.
"Be brave like me," said Louis. "Just smile at them,
and before you know it, someone will say hello."

Louis and his monster practiced smiling.

"What is he?" asked Lola.

"He's my monster," answered Louis
in a little voice.

"Does he bite?" she asked.

Louis shook his head.

Lola asked if she could hug the monster.
Louis and his monster nodded.

"He's nice and cuddly." Lola giggled.
"Do you want to play on the see-saw?"
Louis and his monster nodded again.

When it was time to go home, Lola shouted, "Bye-bye Louis and Louis's monster. See you tomorrow!"

They had made a friend. "You see, my monster," said Louis, "that wasn't so hard, was it?"

When they got home, Louis couldn't believe his eyes.
His new bedroom looked fantastic, and best of all . . .
there were two beds!

"I thought you might need a bed for that monster,"
said Louis's dad.

"You mean MY monster," said Louis.

"Or, you might want to have a friend stay the night,"
suggested his mother.

"Oh, yes!" interrupted the monster. "If our new friend Lola comes to stay, I don't mind sleeping under Louis's bed. I like it there, anyway!"

Before bedtime, Louis
and his monster celebrated
with a jumping contest . . .

. . . and though Louis jumped high, his monster won!